LIGHT BULBS EXTRACTED FROM SNAKE

A 4-foot pine snake that swallowed two light bulbs has a bright future now that it's undergone surgery to have the bulbs removed.

A farmer found the unlucky snake with two lumps in its stomach . . . and immediately knew what the problem was.

From a newspaper article by *The Associated Press*

Published by the Penguin Group
Penguin Putnam Inc., 375 Hudson Street, New York, New York 10014, U.S.A.
Penguin Books Ltd, 27 Wrights Lane, London W8 5TZ, England
Penguin Books Australia Ltd, Ringwood, Victoria, Australia
Penguin Books Canada Ltd, 10 Alcorn Avenue, Toronto, Ontario, Canada M4V 3B2
Penguin Books (N.Z.) Ltd, 182-190 Wairau Road, Auckland 10, New Zealand

Penguin Books Ltd, Registered Offices: Harmondsworth, Middlesex, England

First published in the United States of America by HarperCollins, 1991
Published in a Puffin Easy-to-Read edition, 1998

9 10 8

Copyright © Mavis Smith, 1991
Revised text copyright © Harriet Ziefert, 1998
All rights reserved
Produced by Harriet Ziefert, Inc.

CIP data is available upon request from the Library of Congress.

Puffin Easy-to-Read ISBN 978-0-14-038813-8

Puffin® and Easy-to-Read® are registered trademarks of Penguin Putnam Inc.

Printed in the United States of America

Reading Level 2.1

A SNAKE MISTAKE

by Mavis Smith

PUFFIN BOOKS

Farmer Henry's chickens were not
laying enough eggs.
So he looked in a book for help.
"Chickens will lay more eggs
if you put fake eggs in their nests,"
he read.

Farmer Henry found a box of light bulbs.
"These old bulbs will make
good fake eggs," he said.

"I hope this helps," said Farmer Henry.
"I want eggs—lots of them."

Jake, the snake, wanted eggs too.

Jake went into
the chicken coop.

Jake opened his mouth wide and . . .

swallowed one egg, then another.

Farmer Henry heard the chickens:
Cluck! Cluck! Cluck-cluck! Cluck-cluck!
He ran out of his house
as fast as he could.

"You look like one sick snake!"
said Farmer Henry.
"But you should not have been
in my chicken coop!"

Farmer Henry put Jake down
and started back toward the house.
But he soon turned around.

He could not let Jake just lie there.
He picked the snake up and said,
"I will take you to the animal hospital.
Maybe the doctors will know
what to do."

Farmer Henry put Jake on the table.
The doctors looked at him.

"Very odd," said the first doctor.
"Hmmm," said the second doctor.

They took an x-ray.
"Very odd," said the first doctor.
"Hmmm," said the second doctor.

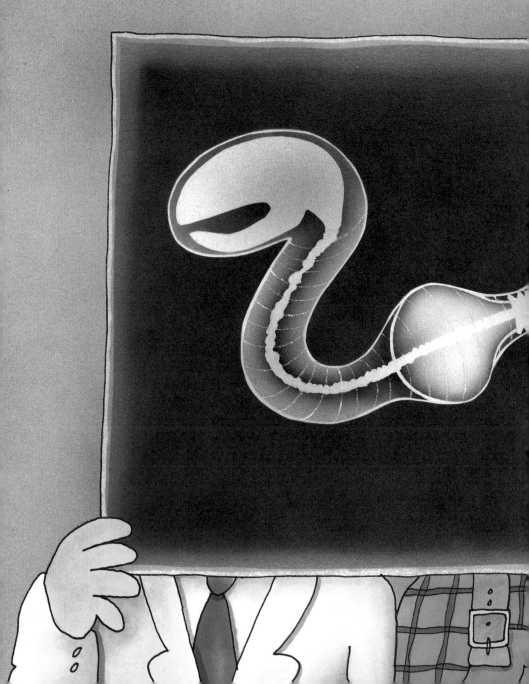

"We must operate right away!"
they said together.

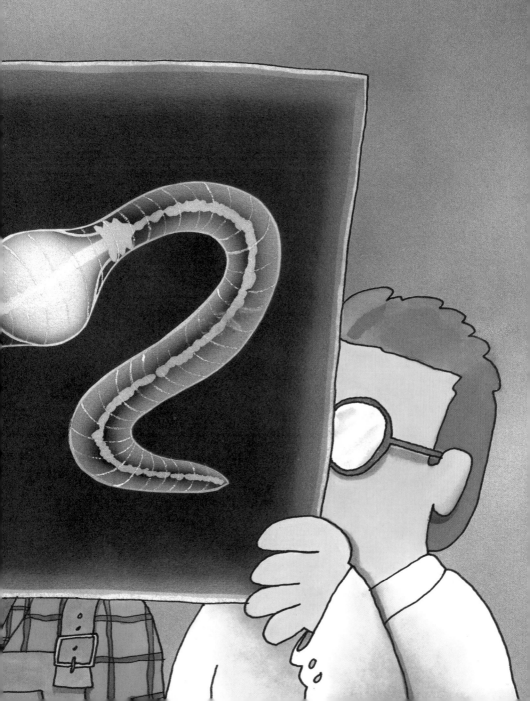

Farmer Henry waited a long time outside the operating room.

He read and played cards.
And he thought about Jake.

Finally, a doctor came out.
"Is Jake all right?" Farmer Henry asked.

"He's all right now," said the doctor. "We operated on him before the light bulbs broke inside his stomach."

Farmer Henry followed the doctor.
Jake was lying in a special box.
"I meant to fool the chickens,"
said Farmer Henry. "But not Jake!"

"Do not worry about him," said the doctor.
"He will be all right in a few days."

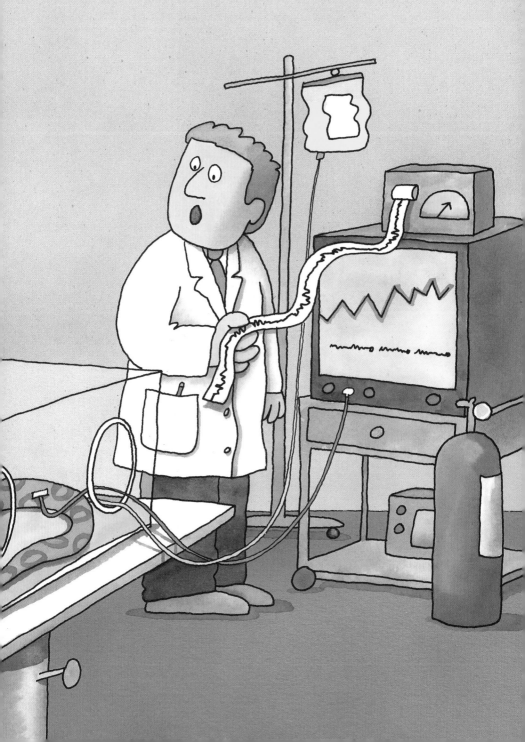

And Jake was!

"He is as good as new," the doctors said.
"And here is a little present for you."

Farmer Henry gave a big party.
Welcome home, Jake!

SCIENCE FUN

1. *A Snake Mistake* is based on a true story. Tell or write a true story about an animal. If you like, draw pictures and make your own storybook.

2. There are nearly three thousand different kinds of snakes. How many kinds do you know? Make a list. Then use a book about snakes to find the names of ten more.

3. Draw pictures of your favorite snakes from the list. Learn some facts about them. You may even want to make a snake picture book of your own.